DAIRY

by Robin Nelson

first step nonfiction

Lerner Publications Company · Minneapolis

We need to eat many different foods to stay **healthy**.

We need to eat foods in
the **dairy** group.

Dairy foods are made of milk.

Dairy foods give us **calcium**.

Dairy foods give us strong bones.

Dairy foods give us healthy
teeth.

We need two **servings** of dairy foods each day.

We can drink milk.

We can eat yogurt.

We can eat cottage cheese.

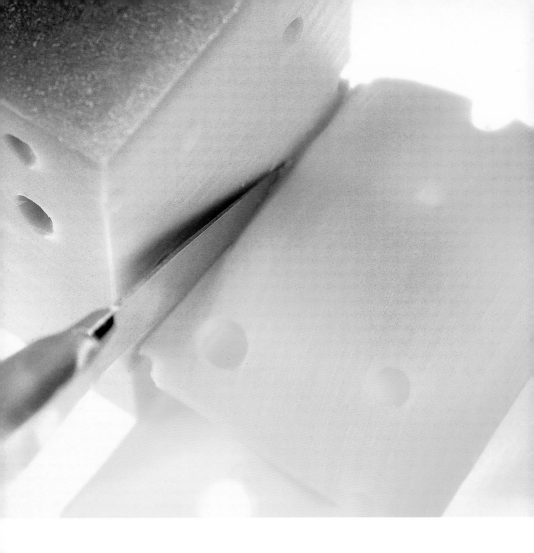

We can eat swiss cheese.

We can eat cheddar
cheese.

We can eat mozzarella
cheese.

We can eat cream cheese.

We can eat frozen yogurt.

Dairy foods keep me healthy.

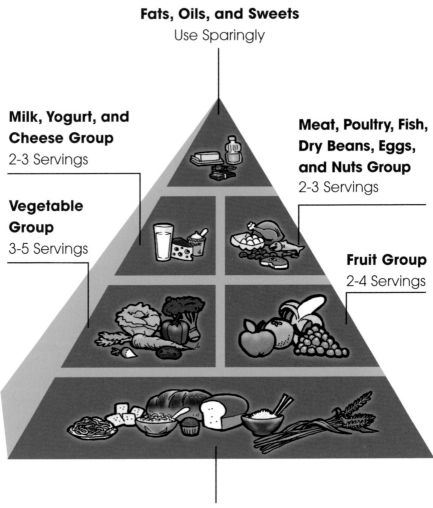

Fats, Oils, and Sweets
Use Sparingly

Milk, Yogurt, and Cheese Group
2-3 Servings

Meat, Poultry, Fish, Dry Beans, Eggs, and Nuts Group
2-3 Servings

Vegetable Group
3-5 Servings

Fruit Group
2-4 Servings

Bread, Cereal, Rice, and Pasta Group
6-11 Servings

Milk, Yogurt, and Cheese Group

The food pyramid shows us how many servings of different foods we should eat every day. The milk, yogurt, and cheese group is on the third level. The foods in this group are called dairy products. You need 2–3 servings of dairy products every day. You could drink a cup of milk or eat a slice of cheese. Dairy products are good for you because they have calcium. Calcium gives you strong bones and teeth.

Dairy Facts

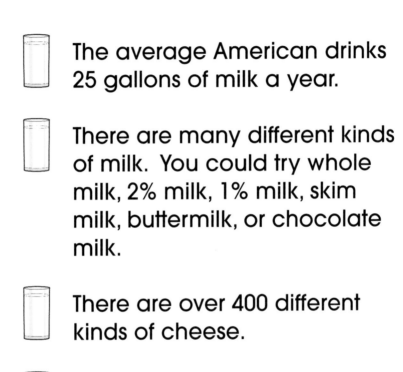

The average American drinks 25 gallons of milk a year.

There are many different kinds of milk. You could try whole milk, 2% milk, 1% milk, skim milk, buttermilk, or chocolate milk.

There are over 400 different kinds of cheese.

A cow must drink 2 gallons of water to make one gallon of milk.

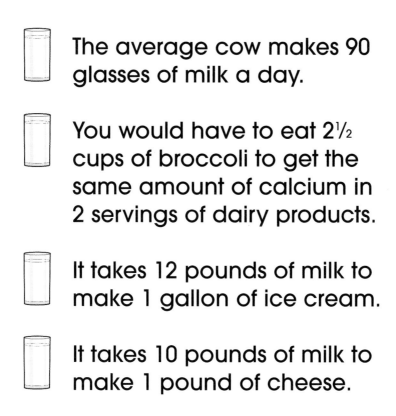

The average cow makes 90 glasses of milk a day.

You would have to eat 2½ cups of broccoli to get the same amount of calcium in 2 servings of dairy products.

It takes 12 pounds of milk to make 1 gallon of ice cream.

It takes 10 pounds of milk to make 1 pound of cheese.

Glossary

 calcium – helps build and repair bones and teeth

 dairy – foods made from milk

 healthy – not sick; well

 servings – amounts of food

Index

The photographs in this book are reproduced through the courtesy of: © Todd Strand/Independent Picture Service, front cover, pp. 2, 5, 8, 10, 11, 13, 14, 15, 16, 22 (top, bottom); © Milch & Markt, http://www.milch-markt.de, pp. 3, 9, 12, 17; © Mitch Hrdicka/PhotoDisc Royalty Free, pp. 4, 22 (second from top); © Amos Morgan/PhotoDisc Royalty Free, p. 6; © EyeWire/Royalty-Free, pp. 7, 22 (second from bottom).

The illustration on page 18 is by Bill Hauser.

Lerner Publications Company
A division of Lerner Publishing Group
241 First Avenue North
Minneapolis, MN 55401 USA

Website address: www.lernerbooks.com

Library of Congress Cataloging-in-Publication Data

Nelson, Robin, 1971–
    Dairy / by Robin Nelson.
        p.   cm. — (First step nonfiction)
    Includes index.
    Summary: An introduction to different dairy products and the part they play in a healthy diet.
    ISBN: 0–8225–4632–9 (lib. bdg. : alk. paper)
    1. Dairy products—Juvenile literature. [1. Dairy products. 2. Nutrition.] I. Title.
    II. Series.
    TX377 .N45 2003
    641.3'7—dc21   2002013614

Manufactured in the United States of America
1 2 3 4 5 6 – JR – 08 07 06 05 04 03